notes on being human

a collection of microfiction

Barbara Brutt

Barbara Brutt

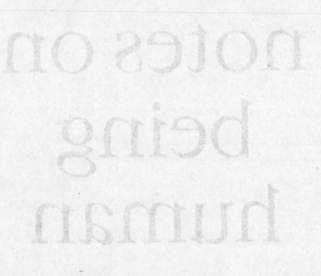

First paperback edition July 2022

ISBN: 978-1-958493-00-7

Cover and Layout Design by Erin Heizelman

To tears, to laughter, to the human existence—
to the people who make it all worth it

introduction

Each tiny fiction was first handwritten into a beautiful notebook over a span of three years.

The tiny fictions grew from a turn of phrase that someone said aloud or that I read in another book. It was a wonderful challenge to find writing prompts from the real world, and I imagine that a few of these scenes would easily translate into a larger story. A few exist as longer versions on barbarabrutt.com.

As you read, I invite you to sit with the emotions that the stories evoke in you, or don't—whatever you need most.

Each tiny fiction is shorter than a short, short story, and you could easily read all of them in an hour. If that's your cup of tea, please do, but I imagine these tiny glimpses of life sipped one at a time.

Most of all, I hope you read these tiny fictions while you pee.

introduction

Each tiny fiction was first hand-written into a beautiful notebook over a span of three years.

The tiny fictions grew from a turn of phrase that someone said aloud or that I read in another book. It was a wonderful challenge to find writing prompts from the real world, and I imagine that a few of these scenes would easily translate into a larger story. A few as longer version or baby version or...

As you read, I invite you to sit with the emotions that the stories evoke in you, or don't—whatever you need most.

Each tiny fiction is shorter than a short story, and you could easily read all of them in an hour. If I as you can of tea, please do but I imagine these tiny glimpses of life sipped one at a time.

Most of all, I hope you read these tiny fictions while you pee.

acknowledgments

Every published work requires a team, and I couldn't do it without YOU and so many others. If you're here, I want to thank you so much for choosing to spend your time reading these tiny fictions—every single tiny fiction is close to my heart and so, therefore, are you.

Thank you so much to my brother, Jonathan Brutt, who encouraged me to assemble these stories into a collection and then pushed me to record them for a short audiobook. He voiced some of the characters! I'd also like to thank Nancy, Karen, Jonathan, Robert, Erin, and many Instagrammers for reading through these stories either in real time or in preparation for this collection.

And to Danielle Martin, who rearranged and puzzle-pieced the tiny fiction collection into an order that feels like an overarching story, I owe so many thanks because it was not a problem that I wanted to solve! Thank you for creating the story order for this published book!

Thank you to Jenly for helping me brainstorm another batch of great title options and to my email newsletter crew for helping me finalize the title. And another thank you goes out to my last-minute proofreaders: Justine James, Jessica Brubach, and Rachel Moeser!

A huge shout-out goes to Erin Heizelman, who has been one of my biggest supports in this author journey with her Alpha reads! It was so good to finally have you design a book cover for me with your graphic design mastery.

If you enjoyed this tiny fiction collection, please review on Amazon and Goodreads, and I would absolutely love if you introduce yourself on Instagram (I'm at @cordiallybarbara) and sign up for my newsletter on *barbarabrutt.com*!

the art of being human

"Do you know what it's like to realize that you live your life on everyone else's terms but your own?" Tears welled up in Talia's eyes, making her green eyes sparkle like a forest in a rainfall. She placed her purple teapot onto the stovetop and turned on the burner. "Someone told me that purple should be my favorite."

I gulped down the desire that welled up in me—I longed to set my friend's life back to rights and just make it better.

"I'm finally asking myself what I want, what I like, and how I want to live."

Her words poked me with a bit of fear. A question pressed against my lips, and as the teapot's whistle screeched through the air, I asked. "Do I get to stay in your life?"

Her eyes snapped up to me. "I don't know."

"You don't know."

"I don't know."

My hand reached for the tea box, and I chose the tea we'd always sipped together, freezing when I realized that maybe she'd never liked this tea. Wordlessly, I lifted the tea bag toward her, and she gave me a quick nod. Plopping the tea bags into the mug felt like a breath release.

2

unzip
my skin

step out
walk away from me

no! no.
i can't do that.
gather me to me
because
i can't abandon me

unzip
my skin

step out
walk away from me

no! no.
i can't do that.
gather me to me
because
i can't abandon me

words absorbed through skin

The first time I wrote on my arm, I couldn't believe my eyes as the ink faded away. So, I tried again, inking the answers to my physics exam on my skin. Only to disappear.

When I turned eighteen, I tried stronger ink and more pain. I wanted, "You are your own." on my skin. It held for a day. And then, it absorbed into my skin too.

But I noticed something.

The words absorbed through skin stayed with me. Every school note, phone number, random wish rooted in my being. They became a part of me.

I threw away my journals. I etched my life story to my veins, and I trekked my heart hopes across my skin.

words absorbed
through skin

The first time I wrote on my arm, I couldn't believe my eyes as the ink faded away. So, I tried again inking the answers to my physics exam on my skin. Only to disappear.

When I turned eighteen, I tried stronger ink and more pain. I wanted, "You are your own," on my skin, to hold for a day. And then, it absorbed into my skin too.

But I noticed something.

The world absorbed through skin stayed with me. Every school note, phone number, random wish rooted in my being. They became a part of me.

I threw away my journals. I etched my life story to my veins, and I tracked my heart hopes across my skin.

i love broken things

"What is this place?" Eliza asked her brother, Peter, as they stood with jaws dropped, staring at the wild menagerie of windmills flying high in a tree, wind chimes embedded in the dirt, and garden gnomes clustered around a bird pond. They'd never seen anything like this before, and they'd lived more places than Peter could count.

"I don't know, but we should go," Peter whispered. "Daddy wouldn't like it."

A sing-song voice bounced into their hearing. It came from behind the tree, growing louder. "I love broken things. Broken things are what I love."

A woman with perfectly smooth hair and a big grin came into view. "Oh, hello! Do you come with broken things?"

Eliza and Peter looked at each other, and Eliza did what older sisters do. She answered. "No, but we just moved in down the road."

"Oh, bother." The lady came over and peered very closely at them. "Ah, but maybe you did bring something special indeed."

Her soft and sweet smile felt like home.

don't lose your
spark of madness

"Don't lose your spark of madness," he said. It had been a whisper, and my head jerked up from my book. Our eyes caught. It wasn't weird that he'd whispered; we were in a public library.

"It's too easy to do." He wore a tattered sweatsuit, and he seemed clean enough. But the cart crammed full of things told me he was probably homeless.

I nodded, hoping he'd move on, but he stepped to "my" table and sat. From out of nowhere, he produced a stack of books and magazines, sprawling them in front of himself and me. He glanced up to make sure I watched as he lifted a book, flipped it so the words were upside down, then he took his eyes to the page.

"Um, sir," I said. "Your book is upside down."

"But is it?" He whispered back. "Or are you the one who's upside down?"

don't lose your spark of madness

"Don't lose your spark of madness," he said. It had been a whisper and my head jerked up from my book. Our eyes caught. It wasn't weird that he'd whispered; we were in a public library.

"It's too easy to do." He wore a tattered sweatshirt and he seemed clean enough. But the cart crammed full of things told me he was probably homeless.

I nodded, hoping he'd move on, but he stepped to "my" table and sat. From out of nowhere, he produced a sack of books and maga-zines, sprawling them in front of himself and me. He glanced up to make sure I watched as he lifted a book, flipped it so the words were upside down, then he took his eyes to the page.

"Um, sir," I said. "Your book is upside down."

"Isn't it?" He whispered back. "Or are you the one who's upside down?"

doodles outside margins

I didn't expect to like the young man who interrupted my reading and wouldn't let me turn another page. He asked question after question.

And then, on the dance floor later, where all eyes should have been on the bride and groom, his eyes flung fire across my skin.

Like a hero from a romance, he sashayed across the floor, and he swept me into dance after dance.

Hands on hips, arms draped across his shoulders. Lips touching lips. Music. Lights. Hands holding cups. Only him.

"No kissing on the dance floor." A voice broke through the brain fog. "Is this man bothering you?"

I shake my head no. No, but did I just step into my own romance novel?

doodles outside margins

americano: straight to the point coffee

"Tell me straight—did you sleep with him?"

"Get right to the point, why don't you!"

"Well?"

The Americano coffee stood between them on the kitchen counter, like a silent judge.

"Well, what?"

"Did. You. Sleep. With. Him."

"What do you think?"

"It doesn't matter what I think. You either did or you didn't."

"Actually, it does."

"What! It's a fact—you did or you didn't."

"Mm. False. It doesn't matter if I did or not because you already believe that I did. And if I didn't, you'll think I lied."

"Did you?"

"Take your Americano, and get out."

"What did I do?"

"You stopped trusting me."

i didn't enjoy the bitterness of coffee until i met him

"You want to hear this story? Fine. But, pour yourself and me a big mug of coffee. No, no cream or sugar—you neither.

"Oh, no, this story can only be told over the bitter black of coffee. Before, I was the kind of girl who liked more cream than coffee. That girl still exists somewhere, but she's not me.

"It started out like most things do, with a simple hello. But that 'hello' was laced with more 'hell' than the actual place. Of course, who could have known!

"Blonde hair, brown eyes. The legs of a soccer player and the arms of a gymnast. And that self-centeredness was hidden so well—no one would ever have known.

"I'm telling you I didn't enjoy the bitterness of coffee until I met... fine, you can add sugar to your coffee—mine is staying black."

i didn't enjoy the bitterness of coffee until i met him

You want to hear this story? Fine. But pour yourself another big mug of coffee. No, no cream or sugar—you monster.

Oh, no, this story can only be told over the bitter black of coffee. Before, I was the kind of girl who liked more cream than coffee. That girl still exists somewhere, but she's not me.

It started out like most things do, with a simple hello. But that hello was laced with more... well, than the actual place. Of course, who could have known?

Blonde hair, brown eyes. The legs of a soccer player and the arms of a gymnast. And that self-centeredness was hidden—so well—no one would ever have known.

"I'm telling you, I didn't enjoy the bitterness of coffee until I met him. So, you can add sugar to your coffee—mine is staying black."

you embody a circus

His fingertips traced over my skin, sending chills to goosebumps in tiny mountain ranges. I shivered, cuddling closer. He kissed my forehead.

But Allen was not done. He made my body feel alive in ways that I had never experienced quite like this before, and the sweet kindness in his eyes comforted and assured me that this was special to him too.

I held onto his shoulders, sinking my fingers into his muscles, and this was all that anchored me to reality.

Somehow, every part of me seemed like an attraction all its own for our enjoyment.

you embody a circus

His fingertips traced over my skin, sending chills to goosebumps. In my mouth, up, I gasped. I shivered, cuddling closer. He kissed my forehead. But Allen was not done. He made my body feel alive in ways that I had never experienced quite like this before, and the sweet kindness in his eyes comforted and assured me that this was special to him too.

I held onto his shoulders, sinking my fingers into his muscles, and this was all that anchored me to reality.

Somehow, every part of me seemed like an attraction all its own for our enjoyment.

heart expanding

i want to weep for joy
in how your eyes meet mine
seeking to see me
all the parts,
not forceful, but
gentle and kind
heart expanding, breaking open
the space between
pain and pleasure—
the wander
of unexpected anticipation
for abundant more.
hold me
in your eyes
to the beat of your heart

a tangible memory
of intimacy

"I love you." He traced his finger across my skin.

The words licked an old, forgotten wound, and tears slid down my cheeks. I wanted to love him back, but the words choked up in my throat.

He kissed my tears and rubbed his dry cheek against my wet one.

And my tears still came, quietly and certainly.

I slid my body away from his and walked to the bathroom, brain circling those three little words. Across the ceramic floor, our clothes piled—a tangible memory of intimacy.

I turned back to him to see him watching me, and I realized three more important words: I believed him.

a tangible memory
of intimacy

"I love you." He traced his finger across my skin.

The words licked an old, forgotten wound, and tears slid down my cheeks. I wanted to love him back, but the words choked up in my throat.

He kissed my tears and rubbed his dry cheek against my wet one. And my tears still came, quietly and certainly.

I slid my body away from his and walked to the bathroom, brain circling those three little words. Across the ceramic floor, our clothes piled — a tangible memory of intimacy.

I turned back to him to see him watching me, and I realized three more important words: I believed him.

she loved until the toothpaste needed to be replaced

She gripped the empty tube of toothpaste in her hand.

"I told John we'd be at the grill." Her boyfriend stripped in the other room. He popped his head around the door frame. "Does that work for you?"

She held up the toothpaste, "It's empty."

"That's fine. We can get another."

Amanda frowned. She'd never stayed with a guy this long. A toothpaste tube was her timeline for each relationship.

"Hold on a sec." Trevor jumped away, returning moments later with a travel-sized tube. "I try to always have toothpaste on hand."

Amanda ignored the toothpaste and reached for Trevor, kissing him.

"It's just toothpaste."

"No, it's so much more, my love."

she loved until the toothpaste needed to be replaced

She gripped the empty tube of toothpaste in her hand.

"I told John we'd be at the grill." Her boyfriend stopped in the other room. He popped his head around the door frame. "Does that work for you?"

She held up the toothpaste. "It's empty."

"That's fine. We can get another."

Amanda frowned. She'd never stayed with a guy this long. A toothpaste tube was her timeline for each relationship.

"Hold on a sec." Trevor jumped away, returning moments later with a travel-sized tube. "I try to always have toothpaste on hand."

Amanda ignored the toothpaste and reached for Trevor, kissing him.

"It's just toothpaste."

"No, it's so much more, my love."

you were always allowed to touch me

You were always allowed to touch me, but I could never reach you.

Bodies twined together—limbs encircling. Heartbeat ricocheting under fingertips. I pressed my fingers and then palm against tacky skin and hard sternum.

What did that heart beat for? And so, I asked. But you brushed my hand aside, capturing my wondering question with kisses until my mind hazed.

And it was only later that I remembered your heartbeat, drumming against my palm but unreachable.

we remained a we

"I can't promise you forever." She said it to me with such tenderness that my heart skipped a beat.

"Who can honestly promise forever?" I asked. I smoothed my hand across her soft skin, wishing for forever—knowing it might not be.

She held my face in her hands as her eyes filled with tears. "Megan, it's not that I don't love you, but I want to be honest."

I looked up at her as her body aligned to mine. She fit so well. Her tears traced her cheekbones, dropping to my face, heavier and warmer than I expected.

"Do you want to break up?" I hated myself for saying those words.

"No."

"Neither do I."

So for that night, Megan and I remained a we.

love is the greatest fiction

From the moment I saw you I knew I would run. Was it the slope of your lean hips as you strode down the sidewalk? Or maybe, the way your gaze lit me on fire at my very center.

It all felt so... flammable, so temporary. Your heat blazed through my ice, but did you not know that when ice melts, water runs?

And I ran.

i think, once upon a time, i believed in love

"I think, once upon a time, I believed in love. But then, I grew up, and I realized that I was not the heroine of a romance novel nor even a drama."

"But you write such amazing romance. If you don't believe in love, how do you do it?" The interviewer asked.

"Love is the greatest fiction." The author paused, sipping her purple bubble tea. "We are obsessed with love because it's an escape from reality—just as fiction is."

"So how do you write such beautiful stories of love?"

"I imagine what true acceptance would be from another—isn't that what we all wish for anyway? Acceptance?"

"Thank you for this interview. You've given me some great stuff."

"Oh, the last few lines are off the record."

"But, why?"

"Readers need the fiction that I believe in love." She slurped the purple bubble tea then.

---- 17 ----

what if we burn
too fast too brightly
lighting the dayscape
but then plunge to inky nothing
will we still burn
then
discovering softer twinkles
under the smoke debris

it doesn't have to
be this hard

Lila stared at the math problem. Surely, it didn't have to be this hard. She couldn't think over Brittany's words.

"Ian messaged me again last night. And he wants to make everything up to me." Brittany doodled across her notebook page.

Lila glared at the numbers. They refused to line up.

"He's planning something. But I know that he's totally flaked on me before, but this could be it. Maybe he's turned a new leaf?"

"It doesn't have to be this hard." Lila tapped her pen against the math textbook.

Brittany lifted an eyebrow. "Aren't relationships supposed to require work?"

"Some numbers and equations just click better than others, coming to a solution faster."

it doesn't have to
be this hard

Lila stared at the math problem. Surely it didn't have to be this hard. She couldn't think over Brittany's words.

"Jax messaged me again last night. And he wants to make every thing up to me." Brittany doodled across her notebook page.

Lila glared at the numbers. They refused to line up.

"He's planning something. But I know that he's totally flaked on me before. But this could be it. Maybe he's turned a new leaf?"

"It doesn't have to be this hard." Lila tapped her pen against the math textbook.

Brittany lifted an eyebrow. "Aren't relationships supposed to re quite work?"

"Some numbers and equations just click better than others, com ing to a solution faster."

he's not a bad guy, but he's definitely not a good guy

"As long as it doesn't hurt anyone, it's no big deal—besides, she's cheated on me so..." Bryan shrugged then.

At that same moment, an older woman struggled to push her cart of groceries. Bryan leapt up from the bench, offering to help her.

Elena watched, pondering her friend. He wasn't a bad guy, but he wasn't quite a good guy either.

"Aren't you essentially lying to her by not telling her about it?" She asked as Bryan bounced over to her.

He shrugged again. "It doesn't seem to be that big of a deal."

and this is why we can't have nice things

"You talked to her?"

"We talked."

"What about?"

"Listen. We talked. That's it."

"She's not talking to me anymore."

At that, she shrugged.

"You can't do that."

"What?"

"Walk around poisoning people against me."

She frowned. "Care for your nice things."

"Don't turn this on me. You're the one that talked to her!"

"Did you ever consider that maybe she stopped talking to you because of you?"

"You turned her against me!"

"When are you going to start taking responsibility?"

and this is why we can't have nice things

"You called to her?"

"We talked."

"What about?"

"Listen. We talked. That's it."

"She's not talking to me anymore."

At that, she shrugged.

"You can't do that."

"What?"

"Walk around poisoning people against me."

She frowned. "Care for your nice things.

"Don't run this on me. You're the one that talked to her."

"Did you ever consider that maybe she stopped talking to you because of you?"

"You turned her against me."

"When are you going to start taking responsibility?"

people talked about love, but he lived love

Every day, my old neighbor refreshed the birdseed in his feeder. From my office window, I saw him. He helped the widow next door too any time she came home with bags of groceries. Sometimes he cut the lawn of the young couple across the street—they had a child in a wheelchair.

And though I enjoyed watching walkers with entwined hands, I liked to see how my neighbor cared for people more. His whole life lived love to every creature he met.

people talked about love, but he lived love

Every day my old neighbor refreshed the husband in his trade. From my office window, I saw him. He helped the widow next door too – any time, she came home with bags of groceries. Sometimes, he cut the lawn of the young couple across the street – they had a child in a wheelchair.

And though I enjoyed watching walkers with entwined hands, I liked to see how my neighbor cared for people more. His whole life lived love to every creature he met.

love is a gift, not an obligation

"Ed, let's get you ready for bed." The talkative nurse's aide bustled into Edward's quiet room in the nursing home. "After my shift today, I gotta pick my husband up from work, cook for the kids..."

Edward tuned her out as he normally did. After all, he knew he was nothing to her—just another item on her to-do list. He'd seen her with her family, though, and he knew that the complaining masked her deep care.

The nurse's aide ran through their nightly routine, all the while talking about everything she had to do.

Edward wished he was still able to form words. He wanted to tell her to enjoy every single moment—the good and the bad. But, especially the bad.

Maybe he wouldn't be so alone now if he had realized that love is a gift, not an obligation.

love is promises kept

Elliot opened the faucet, water spilled into the pitcher. He watched his own hands shake as they turned the handle. The skin puckered and soft.

"Anne, you'd never believe the morning I've had." His voice creaked alongside the tired farmhouse. Slow steps carried him to the first plant. He brushed the leaves away to expose dirt, pouring water to the soil.

"I dreamed about you again. Running through the woods. Sunshine in your hair." Elliot filled his own glass with the water, taking a drink. Then, he moved to the next plant. His wife loved them all: snake plants, spiders, hyacinths, so many. Some from him. Some from others.

The kitchen door squeaked. And two arms wrapped around him. He smiled.

"Why do you still water all of mom's plants? We can find new homes for them. You don't even like plants."

"Anne did, though."

love is promises kept

Elliot opened the faucet, water spilled into the pitcher. He watched his own hands shake as they turned the handle. The skin puckered and soft.

"Anna, you'd never believe the morning I've had." His voice creaked alongside the tired farmhouse. Slow steps carried him to the first plant. He brushed the leaves away to expose the dirt, pouring water to the soil.

"I dreamed about you again. Running through the woods. Sun shine in your hair," Elliot filled his own glass with the water, taking a drink. Then, he moved to the next plant. His wife loved them all: snake plants, spiders, bromeliads, so many from him. Some from others. The kitchen door squeaked. And even a new wrapped around him.

He smiled.

"Why do you still water all of mom's plants... We can find new homes for them. You don't ever like plants."

"Anna did, though."

when did 'i love you' become a bandage

"I love you." My husband traced a fingertip across my chin as we lay in bed. My skin still tingled under his touch.

"Do you?" I stared at the ceiling. The plaster swirled, and the grooves were well-worn pathways to my eyes. Just as my husband's patterned pleasantries and pleasures.

"I do." His tone made my eyes seek his. The tenor of voice echoed to our wedding day when he'd said those same words.

I rolled on top of him, looking into his eyes, feeling his breath with my body. "Then, why does your 'I love you' sound like an apology?"

His gaze softened. "Because sometimes I wonder if I'm enough."

I kissed him until we were both breathless again.

when did 'i love you.'
become a bandage

"I love you." My husband traced a fingertip across my chin as we lay in bed. My skin still tingled under his touch.

"Do you?" I stared at the ceiling. The plaster swirled, and the grooves were well-worn pathways to my eyes, just as my husband's patterned pleasantries and pleasures.

"I do." His tone made my eyes seek his. The tenor of voice echoed to our wedding day when he'd said those same words.

I rolled on top of him, looking into his eyes, feeling his breath with my body. "Then, why does your 'I love you' sound like an apology?"

His gaze softened. "Because sometimes I wonder if I'm enough."

I kissed him until we were both breathless again.

| 25 |
---

it's a fragile place,
having the strength to say
"no more"
while also holding yourself
gently in the grief
that it's come to this.

28

it's a fragile place,
having the strength to say
"no more"
while also holding yourself
gently in the grief
that it's come to this

you're too pretty to be sad

"You're too pretty to be sad."

"What do you mean by that?" Eleanor flicked her red hair out of her face.

"People like you always have someone waiting in the wings."

"People like me."

"Don't look at me like that—you know what I mean. I bet you that there was never a day that you haven't had boys falling at your feet."

Eleanor crossed her arms, staring her friend down. "I honestly don't know what to think since you've just disregarded my feelings solely because I fit the current social definition of pretty."

"That's not what I—you're blowing this out of proportion."

"Am I? Or am I putting your comment into perspective?"

"What? That pretty people have feelings?"

you're too pretty to be sad

"You're too pretty to be sad."

"What do you mean by that?" Eleanor flicked her red hair out of her face.

"People like you always have someone waiting in the wings."

"People like me."

"Don't look at me like that—you know what I mean. I bet you that there was never a day that you haven't had boys falling at your feet."

Eleanor crossed her arms, staring her friend down. "Eleanor, I don't know what to think since you've just disregarded my feelings solely because I fit the current social definition of pretty."

"That's not what I—you're blowing this out of proportion."

"Am I? Or am I putting your comment into perspective?"

"What? That pretty people have feelings?"

it's not enough anymore

"I never want to be fine again." Daisy flipped her golden hair over her shoulder.

"What do you mean by that?" Anne scrunched her nose, as she focused her gaze on the piece of pottery in front of her.

Daisy lifted her own paintbrush, tracing a delicate line across her mug. "Fine is such a blah word—it's not enough of anything."

"My dad uses 'fine' to describe wine though or a good suit. Can't that be the version of 'fine' you use?"

"No. Fine is a throwaway word that masks how we truly feel. I'll never use it again." Daisy declared.

At that moment, her phone rang, and she answered. "Yes, mom?" She listened. "I'm fine."

determined to understand the truth of existence

Little paws clasped on hard shell, gnawing, gnawing, gnawing. Sitting high on the tree branch, the tiny furry body with plumed tail focused energetically on that shell.

And stop.

Freeze.

A dog running to the trunk of the tree, howling its impatience and desire to snag that fur snack.

The squirrel returns to its nut, gnawing until... crunch. Tiny paw flings free splintered edges of shell, and it bumps the dog in the face before falling groundward. Dog sniffs. Squirrel chews. Dog barks, and gallops to next tree.

Squirrel bounces away, tree branch to tree branch.

tiny stars in the corners of my eyes

"What do you dream about?"

"Probably what others dream about." I ran my fingers across the soft suede of the sofa.

"Family? Children?"

I smiled small at my counselor's questions. If this was all that people dreamed of, I thought it sad. Of course, family. But what of, adventure? Learning? Discovery? I sighed. And I answered, "Tiny stars in the corners of my eyes."

"So, you dream of vision and seeing the night sky?"

If I was her, that's what I'd have thought too. But honestly, I couldn't imagine seeing the world, like sighted people, but I wanted to experience it all.

"I dream of traveling and seeing the world as only few can with smell, touch, and sound."

tiny stars in the
corners of my eyes

"What do you dream about?"

"Probably what others dream about." I ran my fingers across the soft suede of the sofa.

"Tangled? Children?"

I smiled small at my counselor's questions. If this was all that people dreamed of, I thought it odd. Of course, family. But what of adventure? Learning? Discovery? I sighed. And I answered, "Tiny stars in the corners of my eyes."

"So, you dream of vision and seeing the night sky?"

If I was her, that's what I'd have thought too. But honestly, I couldn't imagine seeing the world like sighted people, but I wanted to experience it all.

"I dream of traveling and seeing the world as only few can with smell, touch, and sound."

i wonder what would happen if you drank it... #magicpotion

"Challenge accepted." I reached for the cup and threw it back, waiting for the burn of heat; instead, it bubbled, lighting up my insides. It wasn't hot at all, but it tingled then rumbled.

Something climbed the inside of my throat. I tried to gasp, but I couldn't get a breath. The cup slipped from my fingers, shattering on the floor, and a gigantic burp accompanied with fireworks escaped.

"Well dang. That was my favorite mug," you said.

it hurts

They loaded up the boxes together. He carried the box of books, and she carried the pillows. Just as they had done every other time, she organized; he boxed. Together, they loaded.

Tears streamed down her face as she stared at the brick façade of the home they'd shared. Her pinky finger reached for him, as she'd always done, but then she remembered—this time was different.

He stood at the driver's door, helping her in, and she touched his jaw then—feeling it tense under her palm.

Love still burned under this skin.

But their road together had ended. She wished there was anger or something—anything, but it was just sadness and so much certainty.

tied tight,
a robe is like a hug

She buried her face in the terry robe, breathing in the now-faint scent. She hadn't washed the robe since before, and it was starting to smell like her.

She wished she could bottle and keep his scent forever.

Her snoozed alarm rattled the nightstand again, and she groaned. Another day without.

Another day where she had to move forward, functioning "normally" when nothing felt normal.

No one brought her a morning coffee anymore. And she packed only one lunch each day, fighting tears. When would this pain soften?

She wrapped his robe tight around herself, pulling ties snug. If she shut her eyes, for a moment, it felt like her love hugged her again.

33

cool on the outside
reasonable and fine
peel skin
back to fever
boiling boiling boiling burning
i feel too contained

the dread of loss
almost killed me

Three months of waiting—waiting for you to leave. Every step of the process took time and effort. But you had to go.

You wanted to find yourself.

If only you had that haircut or the tailored dress or this life experience—something always promised happiness.

You counted the days and so did I.

While you saw a cage door, opening, I caught a glimpse of the bars you flew towards. The dread of loss almost killed me, but then, it didn't.

Your opened cage door swung shut, and I was the one uncaged—free.

if laughter was planted, it would bloom bright daffodils

"I never thought I'd laugh again after he left my life." She shrugged, trimming yellowed leaves back. The garden sprawled with all sorts of landscaped beauty except this portion with straggly, long grass-like plants wilting across the dirt.

"Do you remember the first time you laughed after...?" The question came from a younger assistant who sat on a low stone wall nearby.

The gardener smiled. "Yes. On a rainy spring day, a bright yellow daffodil bobbed its head at me from atop a small trash heap in a city alley. And it was so ridiculously unexpected, a laugh surprised me."

She trimmed back some more of the yellowed leaves. "Daffodils are interesting because after they bloom, the leaves need six weeks or so to recharge the bulbs for the future year. I like to think that seasons of death or grief prepare us for richer seasons of laughter."

"Is it true?"

The gardener laughed.

36

I don't regret you

I don't regret you
But I regret when I stopped choosing me

I don't regret you
But can we rewind to the moment your
life was more important than mine

I don't regret you
But I wish I had listened to you rather
than my made-up version of you

I don't regret you
But I wish I had seen
How you didn't choose me

I don't regret you
But what if
We had never met?

i wonder how many of us have memorized ceilings this way

I watched the morning dawn across the ceiling of the living room. I couldn't remember how I had ended up out here, laying across the carpet.

Light highlighted the swirls in the ceiling paint, and if I had been high, I'd have felt like Alice in Wonderland.

The dog shifted beside me, returning to her deep snores. Everyone slept but me. Ever since my first had been born, I'd become well acquainted with this ceiling. I knew it at all shade of light and dark. It probably knew my wrinkles in the same way.

We worried together about everyone who lived under this ceiling.

"Mommy, why are you laying on the floor?"

I waved my 5-year-old over, and she cuddled close and we stared at the ceiling together.

she stuffed herself—
full of life

"What are you doing?!" Angelica yelped between giggles.

"What does it look like?" Lily grabbed another fistful of popcorn and flung it at the sky, causing birds everywhere in the park to descend. Lily twirled, laughing and dancing while tossing more popcorn.

"It's for eating!" Angelica popped a few into her mouth.

Lily skipped back to the bowl of popcorn and scooped more into the air.

"Yes, but it's also meant to be enjoyed! And this is my enjoyment!"

Angelica shook her head, but then she joined Lily as she stuffed herself full of life and laughter.

she stuffed herself—
full of life

"What are you doing?!" Angelica yelled between giggles.

"What does it look like?" Lily grabbed another fistful of popcorn and flung it at the sky, causing birds everywhere in the park to descend. Lily twirled, laughing and dancing while tossing more popcorn.

"It's me eating?" Angelica popped a few into her mouth.

Lily stepped back to the bowl of popcorn and scooped up more into the air.

"Yes, but it's also meant to be enjoyed. And this is my enjoyment!" Angelica shook her head, but then she joined Lily as she stuffed herself full of life and laughter.

happiness was her currency

The wide grin, chubby cheeks—one with a dimple. She waved her small fists and launched a loud chortle.

I stared at the child. This small pile of mashed potatoes that wiggled and giggled and cooed in her mother's arms.

And then, suddenly, she was in my arms. Gooey baby flesh warm and soft against my hands. Looking into her watching eyes, I realized I would never be the same. I pressed my lips together, trumpeting a funny sound.

A tiny smile.

I grinned. And trumpeted again. Her smiles were all that I wanted.

happiness was
her currency

The wide grin. Chubby cheeks—one with a dimple. She waved her small fists and launched a loud chortle.

I stared at the child. This small pile of mashed potatoes that wiggled and gigged and cooed in her mother's arms.

And then, suddenly, she was in my arms. Gooey baby flesh, warm and soft against my hands. Looking into her warming eyes, I realized I would never be the same. I pressed my lips together, trumpeting a bunny sound.

A tiny smile.

I grinned. And trumpeted again. Her smiles were all that I wanted.

it hurts to live when someone you love dies

"I didn't love her as much as I could have." Eleanor curled around the baby blanket, breathing in its scent.

"You did." Her own mother placed a warm hand on the small of her back. She traced a circle.

"I thought—I thought I'd have her my whole life to love." A sob crashed from her, and new tears spilled.

"I'm so glad her heart still beats, and yet, I'm jealous of the family whose baby gains a second chance at life."

"I wish it had been me."

"Mom," Eleanor gasped. "Don't you dare say that. I need you."

"No matter what, it hurts to live when someone you love dies." She curled around her own daughter, feeling her heart beat alongside her own.

it hurts to live when someone you love dies

when did you abandon yourself?

All I can think of is how tiny her fingernail was beside my hand. Her soft fingers curling into tiny fists. Her breath constantly in sleeping rushes of in and out.

So tiny, laying across the hospital bed with cords and IVs stringing from her small body.

And I knew, then, under the fluorescent lights, that my heart lay there too. If her breath stopped so would my heart. Though I would live on, my heart would go with my sweet babe.

That's when I knew nothing else mattered in this world but her.

when did you abandon yourself?

All I can think of is how tiny her fingernail was beside my hand. Her soft finger, curling into my own. Her breath constantly in sleeping rushes of in and out.

So tiny, laying, to see the hospital bed with cords and IVs streaming from her small body.

And I knew, then, under the fluorescent lights that my heart lay there too. If her breath stopped so would my heart. Though I would live on, my heart would go with my sweet babe.

I knew when I knew nothing else mattered in this world but her.

we only have thoughts for the things we have words for

"Sometimes, I feel like I have a rabid animal in my chest—it's caught in the cage of my ribs."

"Tell me more."

"It's like ... frantic to get out and suddenly I can't breathe."

"What else happens?"

"Sometimes my body shakes uncontrollably, like I'm shivering. People tend to assume I'm cold and I let them believe it."

"Anxiety."

"Wait, this has a name?"

"What you describe sounds a lot like anxiety to me."

"I always just thought it was me."

we only have thoughts for the things we have words for

"Sometimes, I feel like I have a rabid animal in my chest — it's caught in the cage of my ribs."
"Tell me more."
"It's like... frantic to get out and suddenly I can't breathe."
"What else happens?"
"Sometimes my body shakes uncontrollably, like I'm shivering.
People tend to assume I'm cold and I let them believe it."
"Anxiety."
"Wait, this has a name?"
"What you describe sounds a lot like the answer to me."
"I always just thought it was me."

you have to breathe

"You have to breathe."

"But I don't want to." Her words forced breath to her lungs. "It's too hard."

No longer was breathing happening without thinking. She had to will each breath, concentrating on the rhythm.

"Breathe!"

She filled her lungs, pressing into the breath and focusing on the rise of her body with the breath.

"Breathe!!"

Air rushed in, driving her motion and momentum. In a flourish, she landed the move, and exhaled.

"I did it!"

"You have to breathe." Her coach smiled.

you have to breathe

the room is not big enough
for my sadness
it shrinks in on me
and I can't breathe
I don't want to breathe

the biggest room is not big enough
to hold this grief
it hungers to eat me whole
and I will let it
consume me

the room is not empty
of people grieving
it holds many
and I feel lost here
lost, sad, but not alone

healing hurts more than the wound

I didn't remember the accident. It had been flashing lights, loud voices, and finally darkness. Waking up had been numbness and then scalding pain tearing through me as though I was ripping in two.

They said I was lucky to be alive, and that I'd regain my life. It would take time, patience, resilience.

But no one—no one told me that healing hurts more than the wound.

Even after a year, I was not "back to normal." People celebrated my recovery and cheered me on. But, they don't know that my hand still shakes when I reach for the car door handle or that I practice yoga breathing on highways to stay calm.

My injuries happened in less than a second, but my healing—I wasn't sure if I had enough life on earth to fully heal.

healing hurts more
than the wound

I didn't remember the accident. It had been flashing lights, loud voices, and finally darkness. Waking up had been numbness and then scalding pain tearing through me as though I was ripping in two.

They said I was lucky to be alive, and that I'd regain my life. It would take time, patience, resilience.

But no one—no one told me that healing hurts more than the wound.

Even after a year, I was not "back to normal." People celebrated my recovery and cheered me on. But, they don't know that my hand still shakes when I reach for the car door handle or that I practice yoga breathing on highways to stay calm.

My injuries happened in less than a second, but my healing—I wasn't sure if I had enough life on earth to fully heal.

we will make it through

"It's like wearing ankle weights that are 20 pounds while being strapped in a 50-pound vest that's too tight. Meanwhile, the path set in front of me is a steep incline." Penny reached for her cup of tea.

"How do you live every day like that?" Penny's friend asked.

"It's hard. Some days I don't want to get out of bed—most days actually." She took a slow sip of her tea. "Another insistent feeling exists deep within me. It's mostly a whisper, but I can hear it."

"What's it saying?"

"We will make it through."

so much grief
in growth
maybe
that's why
they both start with
grrrrr

do not hold me responsible for your life

"Mom," I walked in the backdoor. "I got the pizza and wine."

I rounded into the living room where the television was still paused on the series we'd been binging. What I didn't expect was all of my mom's bags packed. She stood there, looking at me. Her gray hair slicked in a ponytail.

"I thought you planned to stay another week." I clung to the wine bottle's neck.

"Baby, it's time."

I breathed deep. I wasn't ready to be alone again with this loss. "But, but, this is how we grieve—you can't go yet."

"But I already have. You need to let me go." She blew me a kiss and walked out the front door, leaving her bags.

I squeezed the wine bottle's neck and the TV blared loud. My eyes sprang wide, and I was alone across the couch with the remote in my hand.

do not hold me
responsible for your life

"Mom," I walked in the backdoor. "I got the pizza and wine."
I rounded into the living room where the television was still paused on the series we'd been binging. What I didn't expect was all of my mom's bags packed. She stood there, looking at me, her gray hair slicked in a ponytail.

"I thought you planned to stay another week," I clung to the wine bottle's neck.

"Baby, it's time."

I breathed deep. I wasn't ready to be alone again with this loss. "But, but, this is how we grieve—you can't go yet."

"But I can, baby. You need to let me go." She blew me a kiss and walked out the front door, leaving her bags.

I squeezed the wine bottle's neck and the TV blared loud. My eyes sprang wide, and I was alone across the couch with the remote in my hand.

i'm keeping a promise to myself

"I'm keeping a promise to myself." She placed the folded clothing into the suitcase at her feet.

"Do you have to?" Her daughter sat on the bed, pouting.

"Yes, baby."

"But who will tuck me in at night? And make my lunches?"

She smiled then and walked to her daughter, flopping onto the bed beside her. Her mini me giggled. And she wrapped her arms around the little girl.

"Your daddy will take good care of you, and your nana, too."

"But, Mommy, I want you!"

"I know, baby," she kissed her daughter's head, "But if I can't keep a promise to myself, how can I keep a promise to anyone else? Especially to you?"

Barbara Brutt, a born and raised Pittsburgher, spent her growing-up years with her nose in a book. After claiming her bachelor's degree in English, she plunked down hard into a smattering of jobs from shop girl to lead digital content specialist with a healthy dose of nanny and house-cleaner. Flying to new adventures is her favorite, especially on an airplane or aerial silk. Barbara adores ice cream and only buys purses that provide room for a book or two.

Find more of Barbara's books at *barbarabrutt.com/books*.

Did one story touch you more than the others? I'd love to know! Connect with me on Instagram at @cordiallybarbara to share!

Thank you again for choosing to read *Notes on Being Human*. It is one of my greatest joys to share stories with you, and I would love if you'd take a moment to leave a rating and review on Amazon, Goodreads, and any other book-centered website. Don't forget to join my newsletter by visiting *barbarabrutt.com*!